LETTERS OF A SUCCESSFUL T.D.

Letters of a Successful T.D.

JOHN B. KEANE

THE MERCIER PRESS
CORK AND DUBLIN

© John B. Keane, 1967
First published 1967
Eleventh Edition 1987

ISBN 0 85342 824 7

Printed by Litho Press Co., Midleton, Co. Cork.

CHAPTER ONE

Tull MacAdoo, T.D., writes to his son, Mick:

Saturday.

Dear Mick,
There's no doubt that this world is full of gangsters and crooks as you'll find out all too soon. Their numbers grow and grow and it isn't easy to make an honest shilling. The thing to do is to forage between honesty and crookedness and do the best you can.

I pulled a nice one last week. I got word, from a friend working in the County Council, that work on the new road to Kilnavarna was to commence on July 1st. You probably know who the friend is. He wouldn't have his present job but for me. You'd never guess what I did! I got into my car and out with me to Kilnavarna on Monday morning. I went around to the one hundred and twenty five houses, and asked them if they would like to see the new road opened on July 1st. They were very pleased, but most of them (particularly that bloody cynic, Flannery, the school principal) doubted it.

'You're a great one for the promises, Tull!' Flannery said.

I felt like hitting him a lick in the gob. He's the rat who said I was under the bed during the Troubles. Anyway, the new road opened as promised on July 1st and they think I'm a small god now in Kilnavarna. There's eight hundred and fifty seven votes there and I could safely say that I'll get five hundred in the October elections. It was a nice move – I never did well in Kilnavarna, as you know.

You'll never guess who got the job of rate collector. By eleven votes to ten, at last week's meeting of the County Council, your uncle Tom scraped home. Your mother is delighted, Tom being the only brother she has, but of course a scallywag without wife or child.

He's doing well for himself when you consider he left the national school from the fourth class. 'Twas from studying the television programmes in the papers that he learned how to read. He has no Irish, of course, but he learned two or three great sentences from that young Irish teacher out of the Gaeltacht, and the best of it is that nobody can understand him. You must hear him rattling them off some time. You'll be flabbergasted. You'll split when you listen to him. He has the life frightened out of the Irishians here. Not one of them can understand him.

It wasn't easy getting those eleven votes. The party was sound enough but the two County Council Independents were a problem. A present of a tried greyhound bitch fixed one but the other is tougher. Cribber is his name. I think you met him once. He's the cranky, red-haired fellow, who's always on about maternity schemes.

'I'm not a doggy man!' he said when I offered him a bitch pup. It so happens that we'll be appointing a Clerk of Works for the two new Technical Schools in the County and Cribber's first cousin wants a job. The first cousin is a proper scut, too, the same as Cribber, but it's worth it to get uncle Tom the job. Q.E.D. as they say in geography.

Oh, by the way, your request for a tenner is a bit Irish. Is it booze, or women, or both? I'm enclosing a fiver. When I was your age, I worked for two and four-

6

pence a day as a ganger in the quarries, and when I couldn't get work I cut timber and sold it by the ass-rail in Kilnavarna and Ballyfee. Bloody good firing it was, too!

I hope you're studying. This is your third year now and I'm getting fed up with it. If you don't come through, you'll have to come home. I should be able to fix you up as a Health Inspector, D.V., although 'twould be nice to see you a doctor.

Your mother was often better. Tom's appointment brightened her up a bit. I hope he doesn't do any fiddling like he did the time we got him a job as pay-master. He was lucky then. If it wasn't for me, he'd be in jail.

Your sister Kate is engaged to a fellow from Lislaw, a farmer and cattle-jobber. He's well connected, so it should mean more votes. I'm trying to fix it so she won't have to give up her job in the library. The Dail reconvenes in a fortnight, so I'll be in Dublin for a few weeks. I hate the hotels. The food sickens me, most of all what goes for mashed potatoes. There's no flavour off the cabbage or the turnips. I can't stomach tinned peas or beans. There's a good pint of stout, of course; I'll say that for it.

I don't like this caper of yours, sending wires for money. I don't like wires. They frighten me. How do we know but maybe 'tis dead you are, or worse. So cut it out, will you, like a good boy, and for the love of God, do a bit of study or you'll disgrace us all, your-self included.

Your mother is saying a novena that you'll get your exam. If you pass it, I'll let you have a holiday in Bal-lybunion for a few weeks. 'Twould be a great suck-in to that rat, Flannery, if you passed. When somebody told him last year that Mick MacAdoo had failed his pre-med for the second time, he got a fit of laughing. 'No trouble to Mick!' he said. 'Where would he be got?' So get cracking or he'll turn us into a laughing-stock. He has it in for me for years. Don't ask me why, unless 'tis plain downright jealousy. He's well in with the canon and the curates. He knows who to soft-soap. Did you hear he's supposed to be writing a book? If there's one word about me in it, I'll bankrupt him.

I got an I.R.A. pension for Sam Heffernan. God knows, he deserved it. I'm not saying he was on the run or anything, but he's voted for me constantly for thirty years. He got the Disability, too. He said he fell off a bike during a chase from the Black and Tans. The boys all know 'twas off the gable-end of the house he fell while he was thatching it but the poor fellow has arthritis all right and he walks around with a walking-stick now, like a bank manager. He gave your mother a present of a gold charm-bracelet after I gave him the news. That was decent of him. I could name fellows I placed in cushy jobs and they'd cut my throat to-day. There's no thanks in the world these days. I often laugh to myself when I think of all the turns I did for people; people, mind you, that wouldn't give me a vote now if they were paid for it.

> For the present, God bless!
> Is it long since you were at confession?
> Affectionately,
> Dad.

Mick MacAdoo writes to his father:

Dear Dad,
Got your letter. I'm up to my eyes in study. I'll need ten more pounds by return of post for new text books.

I'm really swotting, so I'll have to close now. Tell my ma I'll write to her to-morrow and give my love to Kate. See you all soon.

Your loving son,
Mick.

P.S. They don't say Q.E.D. in geography. It's in geometry they say it.

Tull MacAdoo writes to his son, Mick:

Tuesday.

Dear Mick,
Kathy Diggins is four months gone, maybe five. They say it was some fellow in a blue motor-car from Tralee. Whatever colour the car was, he certainly had a good shot.

Your mother is in bed since Thursday with her nerves and Doctor John says she'll have to spend a month in the nursing home. The change will do her good. Don't ask me about it. I only know what I'm told by the doctor. I invited Dr John in myself. He's not a party man, but he doesn't give a damn about anyone, give him his due.

I got your letter and I'm glad to learn you're studying hard. About your request for ten pounds I'm not so glad. Who are you trying to cod? I sent you £10 for text books two months ago. I enclose £5 and suggest you get them second-hand. Anyway, I don't believe a word of it. And what's this story about a hacksaw? Are you cutting off people's bones already? Mind you don't cut off anything else by mistake!

I met a man here lately who tells me that he knows a lecturer in the college. Could he be got at?

Your sister Kate will be getting married in six weeks to the fellow from Lislaw (Harry Lawless). He's a Protestant but she says she'll get him to turn. She says the nicest wedding present you could give her would be to pass your exam.

The match between Kerry and Cork was a washout. Cork forwards hadn't a clue. Incidentally, I'm off to Dublin to-morrow for the first meeting of the new Dail session. We're sure of a majority for the Reclamation Bill but the Civil List business could be tricky. Never trust an Independent.

He's with you one day and fit to cut your throat the next. There should be a Civil List. I might get honoured myself if certain people died. Flannery, the schoolmaster, for one. He says he has incontrovertible proof that I never fought in the Battle of Glenalee. Incontrovertible, if you don't mind! He's always whispering that he has positive proof that there never was a Battle of Glenalee. Of all the rats in Ireland, this fellow takes the cake. How could he know what we went through? Nothing to do but sit on his behind all day, contaminating the pupils. You heard, of course, what he said when he was asked if he would vote for me in the October elections. 'There's nine candidates,' he said. 'Now, if there was twenty, I'd give Tull MacAdoo my number 20, but a number 9 is asking a bit too much!' I went to Corrigan, the solicitor, to find out if this was actionable but he said no.

I asked you in the last letter how long since you were at confession, but no answer. Don't you know that there is no luck where there isn't sanctifying grace, or do you want to be damned?

Your sister Kate is doing the Nine Fridays that you'll

pass the exam. Don't disappoint her. I hope your mother's nerves will be cured for the wedding.

Sam Heffernan drew his first I.R.A. pension this morning. A number of smart Alecs around here say he doesn't deserve it. 'Twas him pulled the Union Jack from the English 'bus that brought the touring Rugby team ten years ago. Not much, I know, but he did his share before that, too, and he was never an informer like more I could mention.

The new road to Kilnavarna is well under way. Flannery tried to get jobs for some of his supporters but I shot that down quick. Every ganger on the job is a pal of mine, so what I say goes.

I hope you're not boozing and that you're glued to your books. 'Twould be a great feather in my cap if you passed the exam. I wouldn't give a hatful of crabs if you never passed another. I've no worries much about my reelection. With hard work, I'll be returned to the Dail, although it won't do my health any good. You're my major worry.

I hope to get the drainage scheme going here before October, as the Minister is anxious to put up another man with me. He's always mentioning the night you put him to bed after a certain wedding. But 'sotto voce' as they say in France.

Next week I'll be proposing that Kate be left keep her Librarian's job after her marriage to Harry Lawless. As Chairman of the Vocational Education Committee I should be able to swing it. Flannery is also a member and he's bound to start off about jobbery and nepotism.

Your mother will be writing to you to-night and enclosing some money. She wants you to buy a sportscoat and flannel pants and suede shoes. I suppose you'd better wear the suede shoes to humour her. Hobnailed boots I was wearing when I was twenty-two. I hadn't a penny to my name till I got the Post Office here. Mind your books, if you have any sense. We went out with the gun against the British to give your generation a chance. Make the most of it and don't leave us down.

The Minister was asking about you the other day in a letter. It should be no bother to fix you up with a dispensary or a hospital when the times comes. You can learn the Irish from your uncle Tom. He is boozing worse than ever since he got the rate-collector's job. Say a prayer he doesn't fiddle. I might not be able to get him out of it this time. Flannery knows too much and so do too many others. I have a lot of crosses, boy, and my stomach was never the same since the hunger-strike.

Mrs Buckley of Glenappa is in the Bon Secours in Cork with suspected cancer of the breast. It may have to come off. Call to see her the first chance you get. She was never a vote but a few calls from you with a pound of grapes or a bag of oranges or something like that and we'd have all the Buckleys voting for us. I never know how to talk to them but you might, since you're a student. These are the little things that get the number ones.

When you're answering this, write a long letter and give us a bit of news. Your mother is always worrying about you.

Affectionately,
Dad.

CHAPTER TWO

Mick MacAdoo writes to his father:

Dear Dad,
Thanks for the fiver. It will have to do, I suppose. I'm night and day at the studies now and I appreciate your offer of the holiday in Ballybunion, but I'd much prefer Bundoran. It's farther away and a lot of Scottish girls spend their holidays there. Nothing bad intended. Just the desire to get away from here.

Tell my mother not to worry and I hope she gets better soon. Send me £3, will you? I need it to half-sole two pairs of shoes and I owe for my laundry. About pulling the professor here. Get it out of your head. These fellows don't give a hoot about T.D.'s or anyone else. I'll pass in spite of them. Don't forget the £3.

Your loving son,
Mick.

P.S. I was at the Cork v. Kerry game, too, and I agree with your findings. If they had switched McGrath from full back to mid-field they might have won. I lost £2 on the game so if you have any conscience you'll send me that as well. The name is at stake, if I don't pay up.

M.

Tull MacAdoo writes to his son, Mick:

Dublin.

Sunday.

Dear Mick,
As you'll see from the above address I'm back in Dublin again for the new session which begins to-morrow. I'm not feeling too hot at the moment. I arrived in by the 9.20 last night and met that messer, McFillen, the parliamentary secretary. I couldn't very well say no when he asked me to have a drink. Half-past three in the morning when we wound up. He drank two bottles of brandy and spilled two more. He abused the night porter and insulted Mrs MacMell. A good job he's a parliamentary secretary. If he was an ordinary individual, he wouldn't be let out in public with drink inside of him and, a funny thing, he's the man who's always going on about drunken driving.

I'm enclosing the fiver – three pounds for the shoes and laundry and £2 to cover your bet on the match. Why the hell didn't you tell me you were going and we could have met. If you wanted money, you'd locate me quick enough.

I haven't eaten a bite so far to-day. Stomach too upset. I had two gins-and-tonics this morning to get rid of a shake in my hand. Only for them I wouldn't be able to write at all. I'll try to eat something later on. My stomach was never the same since the hunger-strike.

Your mother is out and about again. She should be in bed all the time but one of the girls working in the Post Office hightailed it for England with a carpenter from Kiltubber. I daresay he hammered a nail or two. Not even a day's notice! Looks mighty suspicious on the face of it. However, she swiped nothing. Your mother isn't able for the work now but somebody has to keep an eye on things while I'm at the Dail. She was all for bringing Kate home from the Library, but sure that would be lunacy. I advertised for a girl the day before yesterday. With the help of God there will be a few replies to-morrow or after. 'Tis very difficult to get a really honest one.

Your uncle Tom was off the bottle when I was leaving. I made him promise that he wouldn't touch it for three months – but you know Tom! He is probably hitting it hard again while my back is turned. I'll have to buy a new hat to-morrow. Some rotten whelp whipped my hat off the rack in the foyer in MacMell's and made off with it. There was a pair of gloves stolen, too, from the Minister. This place is a hive of robbers. You daren't shut your eyes or turn your back for a minute. The Minister's secretary had a typewriter whipped out of his car last week.

The elections are drawing near. I'll start my campaign in earnest when this session ends. Stay stuck to your books and, who knows, you might wind up a Minister for Health some day. 'Twould drive Flannery out of his mind. He was in the Post Office before I left for Dublin and he asked if you were studying. I didn't like the way he asked it, so I didn't answer him. He has awful bloody neck to come in at all.

'Are you going up for the new session?' he asked me.

I made him no answer to that, either. There's a catch to all his questions. I've that much off by heart about him.

'By Gor, Tull, you're a patient man,' he said. 'Twenty five years in the Dail and never a hum or a haw out of you. The opposition will all drop dead if you ever say anything!'

He was gone before I could come outside the counter.

I got a letter last week asking me if I would address the Yeats' Society in Kilnavarna. I'd swear he was behind it. He's an insulting scut, but he'll go too far one of these days.

The first session to-morrow should be lively, but we have a strong majority. Even the Independents are behind us. We should see the final stage of the Reclamation Bill before the end of the week and then there's the business of the Civil Honours List. You could be on that list some day if you study hard enough. Excuse me – but it has just come over the Tannoy that I'm wanted on the 'phone.

I've just got word from your mother that old Mayney Haggerty is dead. What a time she picked, and the Dail opening to-morrow. That means that I'll have to go down to Tourmadeedy this very evening and motor up again first thing in the morning. I wouldn't mind but I've a sick head that's ticking like a time-bomb.

There's bound to be a wake there to-night and I'll have to put in an appearance. 'Twould cost me fifty number ones if I didn't show up but, by God, although I've done a lot of things in my time, I've never missed a funeral. Here's a bit of free advice for you. If you must go to a funeral, make sure you're seen at it. Go well up in front of the hearse and look as solemn as if 'twas your own mother that was being put under. Better still, put in an appearance at the wake and drink porter out of cups the same as the boys. They like that. 'God,' they'll say, 'isn't poor oul' MacAdoo the fine soul, drinkin' his cup o' porter there in the corner the same as the rest of us!'

Mass cards are vitally important, too. It's the Mass cards they remember when the corpse is rotten in the grave.

There's a priest here on the Quays and he'll sign four Mass cards for a quid. That's only five bob a twist. Well worth it.

I was thinking for a second of asking you to come up from Cork to the funeral, too, but the journey's too long and it wouldn't be right at the height of your studies. 'Twould look well, of course, if the two of us were seen there together, but it's out of the question. Send a telegram, and don't forget it! I told your mother to ring Kate. Kate is as cute as a pet fox at funerals.

I'd better conclude now if I'm to get started for home. Write to your mother. She's expecting it and, for the love of God, for once in your life try to answer a letter without a demand for money. Your digs are paid and you get your two quid allowance every Monday morning. I don't see what you want more for, unless 'tis booze.

Look after yourself and God bless.

Affectionately,

Dad.

Mick MacAdoo writes to his father:

Wednesday night.

Dear Dad,

I trust you got back safely from Mayney Haggerty's funeral. I sent the telegram, and I went to see Mrs Buckley of Glenappa. I took her a pound of grapes. The telegram cost five and three and the grapes cost five bob. I had to take a taxi to the hospital because I hadn't time to wait for the bus. The taxi was four and six, and you ask me not to write for money. Where am I to get it

17

from unless 'tis you, or do you want me to swipe it? I badly need six quid as soon as you can send it. I need four for fees and two for meals out while the exam is on. You make me laugh when you ask me if I'm boozing. Boozing – on £2 a week!

What's this you say about hunger-strike? I never knew you to be on hunger-strike. I'm writing to my mother to-night. Don't forget the 6 quid.

Your loving son,
Mick.

Tull MacAdoo writes to his son, Mick:

Dublin.

Tuesday.

Dear Mick,
Enclosed find a cheque for £6 as requested. I've only just come back from the funeral. I missed the entire first day's business of the Dail on account of it, but so did the opposition man. He waited for the funeral, too; acting under instructions, I would say. I expected a rap from the Minister but when I pointed out my reasons, I was excused. He knows the value of funerals.

Do I detect a certain note of sarcasm in your request to know more about the hunger-strike? You don't know what we went through, boy; sleepless nights, no resting place, our lives constantly in danger.

The hunger-strike took place during the Civil War when every farmer's boy and discontented bastard in the country wanted to be another Michael Collins or Cathal Brugha. Myself and Mick (Razzy) Ferriter were cycling with dispatches from Ballymoney to Kil-

18

tubber, when we were captured by the enemy. There were twenty of them and an officer. The officer pointed a Webley at my head when I started to eat the dispatches and told me that if I didn't spit them out he'd let me have it.

I was terrified, said the Act of Contrition – the short Act as I hadn't much time – but I swallowed the dispatches and so did Razzy. One of the enemy, a fellow called Spud Gerraty from Faha, pulled an open razor out of his kitbag and wanted to cut me open but the officer gave him a kick on the shin and told him he'd get a court-martial. I know many who were castrated by drunken perverts. Maybe they were lucky. Did you ever see a bullock that wasn't content and happy.

They took us to their headquarters and tied us up. They left us in a small room with no light for a whole day. They then brought us out and questioned us about the contents of the dispatches. They bullied us and shoved us around but we held firm. They then took us to a sort of mess-hall where about a score of men were seated at a long table. An orderly served them with boiled corned beef and turnips. The corned beef was lean and the turnips were steaming hot. Our mouths watered at the sight of them. I swear I'll never forget them as long as I live.

We pointed out to the officer that we had nothing to eat for twenty-four hours and that we had certain rights as prisoners-of-war. I wouldn't like to tell you the answer the enemy gave us. Spud Gerraty, the bully who wanted to cut us open, put his plate under my nose and, when I tried to take a bite of the meat, he knocked me over with a push into the chest. 'Twas then that Razzy and I decided to go on hunger-strike.

After a while the officer asked us if we wished to go to the toilet.

'For what?' says Razzy. 'We have nothing inside of us.'

Spud Gerraty gave Razzy a kick in the hip for giving guff to the officer and when Razzy tried to kick back, Gerraty fired a pewter pint at him and flattened him out. They offered us cold spuds that night but·we refused. They brought us hot soup and baker's bread in the morning but we refused to touch it, although our tongues were hanging out by this time. At dinner time they brought us mashed potatoes and fried eggs but we turned it down. That was real will power, boy.

The following night Spud Gerraty arrived with two cases of pot-still whiskey he fecked somewhere. They fell at it and after about an hour they were all staving drunk, puking and piddling all over the place.

The officer was off somewhere with a woman and there was no one sober enough to take charge. They started a sing-song – filthy songs like 'The Wooden Bucket' and 'The Ball O' Yarn.'

They fell into a drunken sleep after a while and we crawled, over their bodies, out the front door. We got on our feet and darted away across the fields. After about two hours, weak and half-blind, we arrived at the house of a widow who was friendly to Razzy. She cut the thongs which bound our hands and put down a pot of spuds and a wedge of bacon for us. We ate it like dogs before it was half-cooked but we regretted it after and got sick, but we had the good of it for a while. My stomach was never the same afterwards. Let me eat bacon now and you'll hear growling and grumbling inside me like a kennel of bulldogs. The widow has a military pension now and she buried two more husbands since then. They were the lucky turnips to her. Spud Gerraty was blown up a month afterwards at the Scrohane ambush. There's a monument to him in Scrohane. Razzy met him fair and square in the belly with a grenade and his guts were draped like ribbons around the bushes. Civil wars is a curse.

So now you know about the hunger-strike. 'Twas no fun. Razzy died a few years after that in Philadelphia. He was in the rats before he died. He took to the booze and couldn't leave it alone. They say 'twas his conscience that bothered him for the way he killed Spud Gerraty. Anyway, he developed pleurisy and died. Pleurisy is the scourge of all boozers. The tubes won't stand up to it.

Your uncle Tom broke out again at Mayney Haggerty's wake, and had to be lifted into a car and taken home.

Your mother is gone back to bed as a result, but Kate is staying on at Tourmadeedy for a few days. I got her a certificate, so she'll be around for a week at least. We'd be in Queer Street only for the certs.

Our friend, Flannery, was at the funeral, too, and what do you think he said to me inside in the graveyard?

'Don't take it too hard, Tull. We musn't break down!'

'Go to hell!' I told him.

I'd half a mind to knock him over a grave and hammer the daylights out of him. He'll say the wrong thing one of these days and then I'll make my move. I'm glad you're writing to your mother. She could do with a bit of cheering up.

I have a long week ahead of me. I have several chores in the Department of Lands about drainage grants and there's two Widows' Pensions to be hurried up. Also there's a nasty case of drunken driving. A young fellow from Kilnavarna knocked a woman off her bicycle and crashed his father's car into the pier of a gate. A few fellows drawing stamps were caught working by an Inspector in Tourmadeedy and that will take a bit of squaring. It all depends on the Inspector. Some of the young Inspectors are tricky but they learn the ropes quick enough when they think about promotion. 'Tis easy to bluff them, although I've met a few lately who don't give a hoot about hog, dog or devil. Independent fellows! The sooner they learn that this world can't afford independent thinking, the better. If every fellow thought independently, we'd have a nice rumpus to deal with. You'd never get anything done and no man would be safe in his bed.

I'm sick and tired of asking you about confession. Have you been there or haven't you? Write soon and look after yourself.

> Affectionately,
> Dad.

Mick MacAdoo writes to his father:

> *Thursday.*

Dear Dad,
Got your letter and the money. The exam. starts to-morrow, so this will be brief. I wrote a long letter to my mother last night. Will you send me £2 by return as I need a new fountainpen. I'll be going to confession on Saturday night.

> Your loving son,
> Mick.

CHAPTER THREE

Kate MacAdoo writes to her father:

My dear Daddy,
I sincerely hope that you got to Dublin safely. I know
it's not proper to say so, but I never enjoyed a night so
much as I did at Mayney Haggerty's wake. Wake up
and live – poor pun!

May I say that it was your presence which made the
night. Your sense of humour improves, but I fondly believe that if humour wasn't there in the first place, there
could never be room for improvement.

The amenities at Mayney's did not make for first-rate
toilette and the following incident, which you did not
notice, may amuse you. Like yourself, I had several cups
of porter. (Anything for the cause, Dad!) It was my first
time in the house and I asked a woman the way to the
toilet. She issued elaborate instructions and I wended my
way to the spot. It was overhung from the east by three
bastard pines and sheltered from the west by a declin-
ing fence of poxed box. When the brief business was
but barely concluded, I was approached, one at a time,
by several male romantic mourners who swore fealty to
your good self and to the party. I have the feeling that I
was watched the whole time during my absence from the
wakehouse. However, anything for the cause! Does anyone know where enjoyment lies?

Henry was greatly amused by my account of the wake.
He's really a wonderful man, Daddy. I'll never forget
what you said when I told you he was a Protestant. Do
you remember? 'I don't care what church he is, Kate, as

long as he makes you happy!'

I know I can get him to turn before the wedding but he must think he's doing it of his own volition. You always said I could charm the hinges off a door.

Sometimes I worry about you, Daddy. You work too hard and you worry too much and mother is of little help since she gave in to her 'nerves'. I wish you would let me give up the Library. I could be of immense help here till the wedding. I'm not too sure that Henry will take too kindly to my working after our marriage.

The Lawlesses are proud, you know. There was a Lawless in Lislaw Castle during the reign of Elizabeth I. – or did you know that? You hear landed Catholic families boasting of being on the same estate for hundreds of years but if this is true, it means they changed religions as often as they did clothes. At least the Lawlesses stuck to the one faith, whether it was right or wrong. I remember when I was a kid we firmly believed that all Protestants went straight down to Hell when they died. Times are certainly changing. People are becoming more broadminded but the old prejudices are not completely dead, of course. There are country people who still believe that every Protestant is an agent of the devil.

Now, there is something very important which you must do for me. In fact you will have to give it priority. A nephew of Henry's who has just finished secondary school wants a job. He failed his Leaving Certificate but he's a nice boy. He comes from one of the poorer branches of the family but, of course, they are terribly respectable. Is there any chance of getting him a job in the Bovine Tuberculosis Eradication Scheme or the Insemination Scheme or whatever it's called. He has a turn for cattle as his father is a small dairy farmer (twelve milch cows and a horse). I know it's asking a lot and I realise how plagued you must be from similar requests but if you succeed it would kill any trace of resentment there might be over Henry's marrying a Catholic. Do your best, anyway, and if you don't succeed there won't be any harm done. But please make a special effort in this case.

Come down some week-end if you can at all, and we'll go out somewhere for dinner. Try and get to bed early. I have only one daddy, you know, and I like him far too much to see anything happen to him.

Love,
Kate.

Tull MacAdoo writes to his daughter, Kate:

Dublin.

My dearest Kate,
A thousand thanks for your letter. Yes, Mayney Haggerty's wake was enjoyable, but make certain you mention it to nobody outside of Henry. A wake is a serious matter for the person who is dead. Get Henry's nephew to apply for the jobs you mentioned and have no doubt at all but that he will be a salaried man within three months.

You know I'd do anything for you. You never caused me a moment's worry from the day you were born, whereas Mick has my heart broken. He's like his mother's people: you can't depend on them. I always say a prayer before I open one of his letters, never knowing what trouble he might be landed in, with some girl up the pole or even worse.

Would you believe that, in the three years he's been going to the University, he never once asked how I was feeling or never made a comment on my speeches at the County Council meetings. He never writes that it hasn't been a request for money. There's nothing else in his head except women and drink.

I'm still laughing over your story about Mayney Haggerty's toilet. Mayney is another number one gone under the clay.

When the Reclamation Bill is passed, we should see work commencing on the Awnee River. It will mean jobs for two hundred men from Kilnavarna, Tourmadeedy, Glenalee, Glenappa and Kiltubber.

I'll have a major say in the giving of those jobs. In fact I know the chief engineer for the job already. He's one of our crowd and as gay a man as ever you met, fond of a drop of the cratur. He has a red nose from it. He's from Leitrim. The bill should be passed by seventy votes to sixty four. The Independents are abstaining. If work starts on the Awnee before the October elections, I'll be a certainty to head the poll. I would dearly love to see the expression on Flannery's face after the final returns. It could be the cause of his cracking up altogether.

I hear he has a plan for employment for the Awnee Drainage Scheme. Married men with big families to get the first jobs. Then, apparently, he has a list of young fellows of merit for the machines, timekeepers, stewards and so on. He forgets it was I who was responsible for the Awnee Drainage and he forgets it is I who'll be giving the jobs. Anyway, darling, I'll try to get down for that week-end. I have to write to your mother now, so, for the present, God bless you.

Love,
Daddy.

CHAPTER FOUR

Tull MacAdoo writes to his wife:

Dublin.

Monday.

My dear Biddy,
I trust when you get this that you will be greatly improved and up and around. The weather here is windy at the moment and I have a slight cold in the stomach, windy too. It may be the change of food because McFillen, the parliamentary secretary, is confined to the hotel since yesterday with a bad dose of diarrhoea. He blames the grapefruit: says it was rotten. He's always cribbing about something, but he gave me a bit of good news last night. You may have read in the papers about the truce negotiations in Kuraka in North East Africa. It is expected that a three-man team will be sent from Ireland as observers and McFillen has intimated that I might well be one of the three. I think we should go.

The climate is wonderful and we should be there for a month all-told. We would be flying out from Shannon non-stop by jet and the journey will not take more than five hours. Kuraka, as you know, is situated on the Mediterranean and you will see from the enclosed booklet: 'Kuraka: Its Customs and Peoples,' what a nice spot it is.

You will see from the photographs that the natives wear little or no clothes, so it must be fairly hot. We might go for a bathe although I was never in the salt water in my life but McFillen tells me that the water there is irresistable. So I hope you'll come. God knows I deserve this trip, but no more than you do. It's a reward for my long years of loyal service.

When McFillen suggested my name to the Minister, what do you think the Minister said? 'By God, if anyone deserves it,' he said, 'it's poor oul' Tull.'

Everything will be scotch free, as they say, and McFillen assures me there's a good fiddle in the expenses if I work my loaf. I'll have to make up my mind by Thursday as the names of the observers will be made public on Friday morning. Also, in Kuraka, the observers can make use of special flights to consult with African leaders in Algeria, Ghana and elsewhere, so it means we would see quite a bit of the world. We can see the gazelles and zebras. McFillen says I won't have to open my mouth, as young Carrol O'Dempsey will be our spokesman. He is probably our most brilliant speaker and is a hot favourite for the Ministry when old Peterson, the Minister for Culture, dies, which should be any day now.

I could have rung you up about all this but I know you're in bed and would have to get out of it to answer the 'phone. Imagine me being selected to go to Africa! Did we ever think it thirty-five years ago when I first stood for the County Council, a raw innocent gorsoon with one suit of clothes and no one behind me, save yourself? Did we ever think I'd be hobnobbing with black chiefs and flying around in aeroplanes? Wait until Flannery hears it! He'll collapse altogether. We'll send him a postcard when we get out there.

Mick's exam started this morning and he sounds pretty confident, if one is to judge from a letter I received yesterday. I have a feeling he may pass this time. If he doesn't I'll have to get a job for him. A third time loser is more than I can afford. If a fellow can't pass one exam after three years he'll never pass it.

I fixed that case of drunken driving. A plea of guilty of careless driving will do and the young fellow should get off with a stiff fine and, maybe, a six month's ban.

I met Judge O'Carvigaun yesterday in the dining-room here at MacMell's. He sends his warmest regards. I remember him when he was a down-and-out barrister without a halfpenny in his pocket and his coatsleeves frayed. His father-in-law is a bosom pal of the Minister for Culture and a black party man.

Judge O'Carvigaun has a fantastic salary now and an Oxford accent to go with it. I had to laugh at him yesterday, touching the corners of his mouth with a ser-viette and calling for the wine list. He couldn't afford a bottle of cider when I first met him. I often ask my-self is it right the way these fellows are appointed judges but then I remind myself that the party knows what it's doing and it is not my business to criticize the ac-tions of my Ministers. There are good reasons for all their actions.

I'll close now, Biddy. Write by return to confirm the holiday in Kuraka.

Your loving husband,
Tull.
XXXXX

Kate MacAdoo writes to her husband:

Dear Tull,
You've an awful neck and I inside in my sick bed, ask-ing me to go out to the wilds of Africa where a lion might guzzle me up, or have you no consideration for

the state of my nerves, or is it trying to do me in you are?

I wouldn't be seen dead in Koolacky or Malacky or whatever you call it. I was disgusted by the photos of them black devils without a stitch of clothes on them and their tits all over the place. I hear they're out of their mind for white women and that they cut their throats when they're done with them.

I've always been a good Catholic and a good mother and a good wife and you had no right sending me on them immortal books with naked savages all over them. If the party want to do you a favour why can't they make you a parliamentary secretary or a Minister or send you to America where I could call to see my Aunt Bridgey and her family. I never laid eyes on one of them and what harm but they're always inviting me out there. 'Twould be a great opportunity to see my cousins in Pittsburgh, too, the O'Briens, they're very high up in the world out there, but you never think of that or do you want them to make a right fool of you. No one in his sane mind would spend a holiday in Africa where you might wake up with a spear in your back or a black man on top of you. I read in 'Housewives' Circle' that they sell white women to them sheikhs and sultans and chefs and they're locked up in tents until the day they die. What do you take me for, to expect me to go out there? You know the kind I am? I was a virgin when I married you and it wasn't easy with the country full of half-cracked soldiers and raping black-and-tans.

My nerves have me killed altogether. I have a terrible cross to bear and you make it worse, talking about them black maniacs out in Malacki.

Kathleen Stack was visiting us yesterday. She's a great consolation to me and the best friend I have. Her eldest boy is going on eighteen. She'd love if he could get into the cadets. You did it before for another boy, so I told her you'd get him in. You'd better get on to it unless you want the whole lot of my nerves to go. In conclusion, may God guard you.

Love,
Biddy.

Tull MacAdoo writes to his wife:

Dublin.

My dear Biddy,
Sorry to hear your nerves are so upset. It's a pity you won't come to Kuraka. It's not what you think out there, and it was the last thought in my head to upset you. You know bloody well that I would never do anything deliberately to hurt you. I never deliberately hurt anyone as you damn well know and I only got cross with people when they made full sure to upset me as you're trying to do now. No, no, sorry – I didn't mean that. I thought you would be honoured by the offer to go to Africa.

The part we would be in, the seaport of Kulpa-Buhrein on the Mediterranean, is occupied by white people and cultivated Africans. Some of them are priests and surely you don't believe that a black priest is a savage and wasn't that black doctor in Thronane Hospital as fine a gentleman as ever you met. Didn't he remove your appendix for you and made a grand job of it.

I wish there was some pill invented to make black men white or white men black, some pill to end all this fecking suspicion of people or I wish there was a race of green men to put the heart crossways on the blacks and whites and end all this whining.

What you ask for Kathleen Stack's eldest boy is next to impossible. 'Twas different with the other boy. He had a fine education and his father, Jim, R.I.P., was a man of action in the civil war. Jim was a good soldier. He fought by my side with Razzy Ferriter and the boys at the Battle of Glenalee. He was a devoted comrade and a fine Irishman whose equal is not to be found walking the earth to-day. It was no bother to get his son into the cadets. It never is for the sons of veterans. However, I'll do my best for young Stack, but you shouldn't have promised his mother anything without consulting me beforehand. Some people seem to think that getting into the cadets is apple-pie. If it was the Civic Guards now, I could swing it easily enough. I'm owed a favour from the right quarter and it would be a mere formality. Many's the nervous Superintendent I straightened out and many's the drunken Guard I got out of trouble.

I had another letter from Mick. The exam. finishes to-morrow and he seems quite pleased with his progress. Let us hope and pray to God that he passes. I'm receiving Holy Communion every morning that he'll get through this time.

I heard disturbing news last night. Apparently Flannery is determined to prove that the Battle of Glenalee never took place. It is only my word against his since Razzy Ferriter died. Jim Bennett is dead. Pug Nevin died in Manchester six months ago and Dermont Fiely died in a nursing home in Boston last Christmas. I'm the only survivor.

The world has produced few rats to equal Flannery, but jealousy is the worst disease of all and there's no medicine for it. He must be the lowest and most vile type of insect in the world to-day. He has devoted his whole life to slandering me and criticizing everything I ever did. I'd swear it was he who wrote the song: *'The Bright Young Faces of the Old I.R.A.'* but I have no proof. What has he against me? And why me, of all people? Is it because I didn't pull the State Solicitorship for his son? How could I do that and he an Opposition man? I've nothing against young Flannery but the party comes first. Flannery must think he's God Almighty. He'd never have the school only for the way he kow-tows to the priests.

If duelling was legal, I'd challenge him in the morning and I wouldn't miss. Rats like him are better under the ground.

You never can tell about that trip to America. There's a trade delegation going to New York next summer and although I have no qualifications they might stuff me in. I'll talk to McFillen about it and he'll talk to the Minister, so you may be seeing your Aunt after all and all the rest of your relatives.

I was in the Land Office this morning about the distribution of old Lord Brockley's estate in Kilnavarna. The greed of some people would frighten you. One farmer, with one hundred and forty acres, wants more, but I think my own relations will come well out of it.

Your own is your own any day. I met the Commissioner and we had a booze-up together. He's a Wexford man and has a son who knows Mick in the University.

Your cousin Danny is fixed up nicely too. I saw to that. Fifteen acres of the best of it and bordering his own. I also got ten acres for myself. I have as much right to it as anybody. 'Twas us broke the English yoke.

Lord Brockley is getting well paid by the Land Commission but he insists on holding on to the fishing rights on the Awnee River. I had my eye on those but

33

he knows their value. Twenty pounds a rod for thirty rods is six hundred a year and then there's the netting which runs into £3,000 a year. My idea was to start a company with myself as managing director. We could have bought the rights for nine or ten thousand pounds but his solicitor is a cute buck from Cork. It's too late now and if we went after it, the price would be upped to fifty thousand quid. Another golden opportunity missed, but it can't be helped.

I'm going to go after Jimmy Hassett's farm, the small one on the old Mail Road to Kilnavarna. Keep this under your hat as it can mean thousands in due course. I happen to know that there will be thirty new houses going up there shortly and it would also do as a site for the new School and Garda Barracks. I won't buy it in my own name, of course. Too much talk. I should be able to purchase it for fifteen hundred quid and it should be worth seven or eight thousand for the sites. I have only nine hundred cash in the bank at the moment but it should be no trouble to raise the rest. All I have to do is ask.

I had a letter from my old friend, Timmony Hussey. He wants a job. The only thing I can manage just now is a Hotel Inspector and, sure, Timmony wouldn't know a napkin from a sheet of toilet paper. There are a few weeks' training, so he should manage nicely. He has a big nose so he should be able to smell things.

Some of the Inspectors I know in the racket wouldn't know mutton-broth from dishwater, but it's a cushy job with good expenses. Anyhow, love, I'll try to arrange that trip to America. I hope your nerves are better.

Your loving husband,
Tull.

34

Kate MacAdoo writes to her husband:

Dear Tull,
What do you mean by saying that you want me to go to America in my condition? Do you want to murder me altogether? God help me, I'm in a terrible state. I told Kathleen Stack about the cadets. If you don't get him in I'll never speak to you again. Nell Fetherington is gone to Limerick to have her womb removed. She hasn't been well since she lost her baby. I've great pity for her, married to that half-idiot, Paddy. Nine babies in eight years, although she used to say herself that her annual visit to the nursing home is the best holiday one could get. The Carneys of Kilnavarna were here last night to know would you get them a grant for the extension they put on to the house. I told them you would, of course. I've a splitting headache and so I must conclude.

As ever,
Biddy.

CHAPTER FIVE

Mick MacAdoo writes to his father:

My dear Dad,
The exam. finishes this evening and I am quietly confident. These have been the most strenuous days of my whole life and I'm really flattened. To make things worse, I haven't the price of a butt, my last pair of socks have holes and I have a splitting headache. I would have sent you a wire for money but I know your hatred of wires. I need £5 urgently. Two pounds of it is for a contribution towards a gift for one of the professors who is to retire shortly. I need the other three to buy a new pair of socks, to buy a summer vest and to buy my ticket home this evening. Would you be a brick and wire the £5. Don't wire it to the digs. Send it to myself c/o The Hideaway Bar, Mangolds Lane, off Jug Street, Cork City. I'll explain the reason for not sending it to the digs when I see you. I hope you're keeping well. I sent a picture postcard to Flannery. It represents a fellow who got stuck in a toilet and I got an art student, a pal of mine, to substitute Flannery's head for the real one. The finished product is the spitting image of Flannery. You'd get an attack of laughing paralysis if you saw it. Don't forget the £5. or maybe you had better make it six, as I promised the art student a quid as soon as it came to hand. God bless.

Your loving son,
Mick.

Tull MacAdoo writes to his son, Mick:

Dublin.

Dear Mick,
Got your letter just as I was going to vote on the Civil
List Bill. You'd make a right good candidate for an
Honours List. When it comes to reasons for sending
you money, you are the finest liar I've ever encounter-
ed. That's your real vocation.

For quietness sake I am posting you on a cheque for
six quid. What business have you got in the Hideaway
Bar? I know Mangolds Lane by reputation and it is not
a spot I'd like to be alone in at night. Between tally-
women and Teddy boys a man wouldn't know when
he'd be murdered.

That was a great idea sending the card to Flannery,
but I've received an open postcard this morning, anonymous as usual. There's no doubt at all about the iden-
tify of the sender. It was definitely Flannery and the
bother is that it was seen by several others before I got
it. What do you think the rat is up to this time? He
wants to know: *'Did Bacon write Shakespeare?'* and
asked me if I would address the Francis Bacon Society
and give my opinions on the controversy.

Who is this Francis Bacon? There are no Bacons in
the constituency. There are Beacons all right, but not
Bacons. There is Wilberforce Beacon and his sister
Amelia in Dry Valley, south of Kilnavarna. They
bought Moran's place in 1940. They say he is a retired
Methodist minister. I haven't a clue as to what politics
they have. In fact, as far as I know, they never vote
and keep very much to themselves. If Flannery wants
an argument he should leave religion out of it.

McFillen, the secretary, is a sick man these days. He blames it on bad food but I would say too much booze is nearer the truth. The man has a phenomenal gut for brandy. It's a mystery to me how he can afford it on his salary. Two bottles of brandy a day runs up to six quid. That's over two thousand quid a year and that's his whole salary down the drain. He can carry his liquor, however, and that's the important thing. I was down in his constituency with him last year at the opening of a new Vocational School. He left Dublin at half-past eight and by the time we reached our destination he had twenty-three small brandies thrown back. After the ceremony, the bishop invited us for some refreshments and when he asked Mac to have a drop of brandy or whiskey or something, 'No, thank you, your Lordship,' Mac said, 'I didn't touch a drop with seven years.' The Bishop believed him, because the Bishop said to me later that the country could do with more politicians like McFillen.

It's teeming rain here in Dublin. You'll be glad to hear we carried the Civil List Bill without the opposition we expected, 68 for and 42 against, with thirty abstainers and a few absentees. Cubway, that lunatic Independent from the north, suggested that Paul Singer be the first person to be honoured. He said that any man who could take down the North Kerry farmers deserved the greatest honours the country could bestow. His suggestion didn't provoke the laughter one would expect, which confirms my earlier belief that a number of prominent members were investors. Some of them turn purple when Paul Singer's name is mentioned. I lost a hundred pounds myself, which I invested in Kate's name but, thank God, it was only chicken feed in comparison to many I could name.

Go straight home when you cash this cheque as there are two meadows of hay to be cut and you'll have to keep an eye on the workmen. I won't be down for a few weeks as there is still a lot of business to be concluded and if I asked for a few days off the Minister would have my head.

I look forward keenly to the exam. results. If only you could be lucky enough to pass, I'd be the happiest man in Ireland. Your University education has cost me £920 to date and that does not include the £85 I paid out for your grind before you sat for the matriculation and no exam. passed yet. There's no father but myself would endure it for so long. You have no idea of the value of money. If you had, you would have passed your exam. the first year. However, third time lucky, as they say.

I read in the 'Journal' yesterday where Flannery was re-elected Chairman of the Kilnavarna Development Association. That rat couldn't develop a negative!

There was quite a celebration here in MacMell's last night. Even Mrs MacMell got giddy from booze and wound up sitting in MacFillen's lap. The Minister's wife had a baby boy – the first – and he threw a party. He insisted that I sing a song and I sang: *'the Black Hills of Dakota.'* It's my favourite next to *'The Red River Valley.'* Everybody joined in the chorus.

McFillen took off his shoes and danced a hornpipe at two o'clock in the morning but, as usual, he insulted somebody and there was a bit of a scrap in one of the lavatories. We got him to bed in the end, and, as far as I know, he's presently boozing somewhere down town with members of the Carrigmult Builders' Association who have just returned from Copenhagen. He has something up his sleeve. I should know what it's all about when he shows up.

> Don't forget to go straight home.
> Meanwhile, God bless.
> Affectionately,
> Dad.

CHAPTER SIX

Tull MacAdoo writes to his daughter, Kate:

Dublin.

My dear Kate,
My heart is broken by your mother. I was offered a chance to go to Kuraka, a paradise on the African side of the Mediterranean, but she turned it down because of her 'nerves'. There isn't a man in the Dail wouldn't give his right hand for the chance I'm getting. If I told the Minister that it was because of my wife's 'nerves' I couldn't go I'm sure he would tell me to have my head examined. What a spouse for a politician to have.

She wanted to go to America instead but when I told her that I might be able to arrange it, her 'nerves' seemed to get worse. I can't afford to have 'nerves'. 'Tisn't but I could do with a break but what's the point when she constantly refuses to break with me.

My chief reason for writing this is to tell you that Mick is on his way home. He will probably arrive before you receive this letter. Take very careful note of the following instructions.

Under no circumstances is he to be left behind the counter of the Post Office or shop alone.

Make sure there's always somebody with him or you'll find the cash register acting queerly.

God knows I don't begrudge him a few pounds but he overdoes it and too much spending money is not good for a lad of his age and besides I'm told he has a terrible tooth for porter. The local girls are always throwing themselves at him and he has the antics of a Sultan.

They know he is a good mark should anything go wrong. See to it that he supervises the cutting and saving of the hay in the two meadows. I'm not a slave driver but when my back is turned the men won't work. You know that as well as I do. Oh, they'll drag through the day all right but there's no proper return for the hours they put into it, hours that will have to be paid for whether the work is done or not.

We will never again see a worker like Topper. I will never forget him as long as I live.

You probably don't remember Jeremy Topper. He died of T.B. when you were about three or four. It still plays on my conscience that I might have driven him too hard. In those days we used to get youngsters out of Kilnavarna Industrial School to work as farm labourers. They were usually aged about fifteen or sixteen. You didn't have to pay them much and I know for a fact that most people paid them nothing.

I had several lads but they were better for eating than they were for working. It was a mistake, too, to get fellows who hadn't made their Confirmation because you would have to leave them off every day for catechism.

Jeremy Topper was different. He had made his Confirmation. He was a great worker and a light feeder. He was as thin as a whippet but I never heard him complain and he worked out-of-doors, hail, rain or shine.

I often worry that I might have misused him, but no, that isn't true, because he worshipped me as a son would. He had no father or mother but that was during the Economic War when nobody could afford a regular workman and the dead calves were blocking the eyes of the bridges.

The only labour we could afford were young lads or girls out of orphanages or Industrial Schools. Jeremy died when he was twenty but I think he killed himself. I never touched him, although I know of boys and girls who were whipped and punched like slaves and there were young girls who were badly abused by certain farmers who are pillars of the Church to-day.

May God forgive them and the priests who knew what was going on. I put up a headstone over Jeremy when he died. There was no cure for T.B. in those days and I've lost count of all the handsome boys and girls who died as a result of it, my own brother Dan for one, and my poor mother, God rest her, cut off in her prime.

But to pass from poor oul' Jeremy, the Lord grant him a bed in Heaven, I was with McFillen last night and he came up with a brilliant idea. When doesn't he? It will be a poor look-out for all of us if the booze affects his brains.

As you know, the new housing scheme for Kilnavarna is long overdue and it looks as if the County wouldn't be able to afford it for many a year. McFillen knows how I can get 25 pre-fabricated houses at £250 a house. That's £6,250.

A pal of his will be importing fifty of them from Europe and I can have twenty-five. I'll probably get a friend of mine here in Dublin to buy them and I see nothing to prevent me from flogging them to the county for four or maybe five hundred apiece.

In the name of the sainted mother of God, destroy this letter! Because, if wind of this move got out, I was finished. It would be a front-page scandal. It's a clever move, you'll have to agree. The houses are being imported as an experiment, and, if they are a success, they will be manufactured here. McFillen will be a sleeping director of whatever company gets the concession. If the voters of this country knew one-tenth of the things I know, there would be a revolution to-morrow morning.

However, we are the men who freed the country and we are entitled to certain considerations. Don't forget what I told you about Mick and the shop. He'd have a fiver fiddled while you'd be looking around you. Give my fond regards to Henry. It won't be long more, D.V. He's a fine cut of a lad and, by all accounts, a steady reliable worker. The country can use steady, reliable workers. I wish there were more of them. I'll see to it that there will be a wedding to remember. I have promises from three Ministers that they will attend. Don't spare my purse if you have any ideas which might make the day a more perfect one for you.

Your loving,
Daddy.

Kate MacAdoo writes to her father:

My dear Daddy,
Thanks a thousand for your letter. I'll do as you ask with regard to Mick. Last night I went to see Bridgie Teeling. She's just had her fourteenth child and, believe me, this is a family which is in dire want. Whatever you do you must see that her husband, Sam, is made a road steward. It's an absolute necessity if they are to live any sort of life at all. There are holes in his waders and he has no socks. I made him a present of a pair of strong boots and six pairs of woollen socks. He's been a labourer now for 25 years. Since you first

stood for the Dail he has never voted for anybody else and neither has Bridgie.

Number one, Tull MacAdoo, and no number two's or three's either. I told her last night you would do your utmost and I pray that you will succeed. I really do because I know of no more deserving case.

That was a brilliant idea of Mac's about the prefabs. I hope it goes off without a hitch. Don't worry about the letter. It has since its receipt been consigned to the flames and nobody will ever know what it contained. I agree that it could be explosive in the hands of a hungry sub-editor. You know what they can do as well as I do and there's nothing in the world will buy them off.

Give Mac my love and tell him that he's been behaving poorly for a godfather. He hasn't dropped me a line in a year. Tell him to go easy on the brandy, that I said he was too nice to die – from alcoholism.

Your beloved brother-in-law, my uncle Tom, is off the booze since ere yesterday, but he could be on it again to-morrow. It's a small relief anyhow. I'm at my wit's end trying to get him interested in a girl from near Glenappa. She's going on forty but she's sensible and quite a looker. It might be the makings of him if he settled down.

There is little of interest here just now, except that business is booming in the shop since work started on the Awnee Drainage. Most of the workers cash their cheques here and they spend the best part of them before leaving the shop.

Mother is still in bed. Was there ever a time when she wasn't complaining about something. When 'twasn't her nerves 'twas gas and when it wasn't gas it was neuralgia or laryngitis.

Mick has just come in the door now looking like an

English squire in his suede shoes and sportscoat. I'll wind up now to get all the news of Cork from him. He looks well. In fact he looks downright handsome. A pity he hasn't a brain. I'll end now as he is about to come behind the counter to serve a customer. His willingness to do this surprises me and justifies your cautioning me about the till. Au revoir.

Love,
Kate.

Mick MacAdoo writes to his father:

Dear Dad,

Since I am apparently no longer to be trusted by the members of my own family, I feel honour bound to drop you a line so you can regard this letter as a protest. I am not in the habit of begging and it breaks my heart to have to go to my beloved sister when I want a few shillings. It is with great regret that I take my pen in hand to begin this sorrowful epistle since it is not in my nature to stir up trouble under the roof where I was born and reared. I am, however, your only son and as such I feel that I am entitled to certain considerations. I should, I feel, be allowed to go to the cash register without escort. I am not a tramp or a robber and I think that as the only male member of the house, apart from yourself, I should be in charge and not subject to the miserly whims of your darling daughter. Unless you write and tell her that I am to be trusted I feel compelled to demand £15 from you unless you want me in Court where I will be forced with my many obligations. I regret if the tone of this unfortunate epistle is without affection but I am the blood of your blood and I have my pride. I await your reply.

Sincerely,
Your loving son,
Mick.

Tull MacAdoo writes to his son, Mick:

Dublin.

Dear Mick,
You write a good letter. It's a pity you weren't around in the time of St. Paul. He would enjoy you even more than me. Speaking about saints, I pray for the day when you will write me a letter where there will be no request for money. As for sending you £15, I have no notion whatsoever of doing so. I trust Kate implicitly and I am quite sure she gives you enough. If you would only remember, Mick, that there are other things in life besides money, or can you think without thinking of money? I'll sign off now and trust that you will take note of what I said.

As ever,
Your affectionate father,
Tull MacAdoo.

Tull MacAdoo writes to his daughter, Kate:

Dublin.

My dear Kate,
Rumour has it here that Mrs MacMell is going to marry again. 'Twill be the talk of the city if she goes through

with it. She's fifty-five if she's a day and the buck she's marrying is hardly thirty. He's the private secretary to a Cabinet Minister. He's supposed to earn fifteen hundred pounds a year in his capacity as private secretary. Supposed is right!

McFillen is writing to you to-day. He was all apologies. I think he's gone out somewhere to get you a present of that new perfume: 'Exploda'.

It's very expensive but he's in the chips at the moment – something to do with insurance. It's commonly rumoured that the Minister and himself got a sum of £2,000 apiece for giving the insurance concession on a certain item to a certain company. No doubt Mac will tell me all about it in his own good time. He has the diarrhoea constantly now and, to be candid with you, I don't like his colour. He gets fits of empty retching and I'm after him to see a doctor. When he came downstairs yesterday morning he went straight to the bar and breakfasted on two large brandies. When you're writing to him, invite him down for a few days. He might go off the booze for a while for your sake. He's always telling me that if he had a daughter, he'd want her to be a girl like you.

Seriously, however, he's a sick man and I'm too fond of him to see anything happen to him. For instance, he eats little or nothing and he starts off every day with a large brandy. No constitution could stick that kind of carry-on. If a person won't eat, that person must take the consequences. A few of us here – his near friends – are constantly after him to go and see a doctor but he's so pig-headed that it is a waste of time asking him any more. He spent one whole day last week without eating a bite of any kind, not even a sandwich.

I, myself, still feel the effects of the hunger-strike and, Kate, for God's sake tell no one, but I'm having nightmares again about Dodigan, the R.I.C. sergeant we killed in 1921. I try to dismiss it from my mind but his face keeps re-appearing in my dreams and I wake up sweating. I'm still convinced he was a spy, although his family and friends swear otherwise and maybe they're right. Who's to say in time of war. All is fair, they say, and I hope it's true.

Why would he be playing cards till all hours of the morning with the Tans, and how could the Tans know where Razzy and I were hiding the night they raided my uncle Mick's house in Kilnavarna. Still, I can't get him out of my mind. He must have been alive for hours after we left him on the roadway. Maybe we should have got him a priest. That's the part that worries me most, him not having a priest. I said the act of contrition into his ear after we shot him, but was it enough?

I wouldn't like the thought of going myself without a priest, although I never got on with them since oul' Canon Murkason said we were all murderers. Canon Murkason was a pro-British hobo. Maybe 'tis him we should have shot instead of a man with a wife and three kids. God pity me with these horrible bloody dreams! It is not right that I should be made suffer for only having done my duty.

I hope Mick is supervising the workmen and I hope you're keeping him well away from the till. Judging from his last letter you seem to be succeeding. The results of the exam. should be out any day now. I'll be down in a fortnight to start the campaign for the October elections. Mac has promised me a week at least and he will address meetings at nine venues. He's a powerful orator, the kind country people fall for. You'll have to start writing out speeches for me shortly. Put plenty humour in them and a few good stories. They like that.

I hope your mother is well. I wrote to her three days ago but I've had no reply since. I can't figure her out. She should be the happiest woman in the world. She wants for nothing and she knows I love her but she persecutes me every chance she gets. I don't know how I put up with it.

Don't worry about Sam Teeling. I'll see that he's made a steward but remember that Rome wasn't built in a day. Give my regards to Bridgie and the fourteen kids. The bother is that most of them will be gone to England before they're old enough to vote. Well, darling, I'd better dry up and look after the affairs of my constituents. Give my regards to Henry and my love to yourself.

Affectionately,
Your loving Daddy.

Mick MacAdoo writes to his father:

Dear Dad,
Here, at last, is what you've waited for so long, a letter without a request for money. Does it make you happy. But try to remember that St. Paul had to have money to take him on his journeys. Am I supposed to travel the constituency on wings, or what? The reason I'm not writing to you for money is because I swiped two fivers out of Uncle Tom's wallet when he was asleep up against your manger after a booze which will be spoken about for many a day to come in Tourmadeedy. I could have swiped more but we musn't make pigs out of ourselves. Your daughter is fine. She guards your treasury better than any bloodhound. Your wife has a new disease

which deserves mention in medical journals. I'll call it Crowitis. She resents the cawing of crows in the mornings and says they'll be the death of her. You can pick 'em, Tull.

Cheerio.
Your loving son,
Mick.

CHAPTER SEVEN

Kate MacAdoo writes to her father:

My dear Daddy,
I'm afraid I have rather disturbing news. It has nothing
to do with Mick or Mammy or Henry. All is fine here,
but, since you do not buy or read *'The Demoglobe'*, the
following report will interest you. I am quoting direct-
ly from the leader page:

'LOCAL SCHOOLMASTER TO PROVE THAT BATTLE OF
GLENALEE WAS FICTITIOUS!

*'Mr James Flannery, N.T., asserts that he has con-
clusive proof that there was never a Battle of Glenalee.
In an exclusive interview, Mr Flannery told our re-
porter that there may have been a few scraps there between weasels and rabbits, but there was no gun battle.
There were battles, he said, between weasels and rabbits and murder was perpetrated but it was only when
a sparrow-hawk assaulted a wren. He said the battle
was a figment of the imagination of Mr Tull MacAdoo,
T.D. He challenged Mr MacAdoo to refute his statements. 'I am convinced,' Mr Flannery concluded, 'that
no battle was ever fought there, and,' he added, 'I have
the evidence to prove it.'*
I hate to send you upsetting news like this, Daddy, but
isn't there something we can do to make him eat his
words? If he's not made to look foolish quickly, it
could be disastrous in the October elections. Nobody
believes him, I know, and you might think it wiser to
ignore it, but I firmly believe that he must be shown up.

It has come at a critical time. Twenty years ago you could have shot him and got away with it but not to-day. More's the pity, because a bullet is exactly what he deserves.

It may all blow over, but, on the other hand, it may gain momentum and spread all over the country. You know how people love to see a national hero like yourself brought into disrepute. Ask Mac what he thinks. Mac's advice would be invaluable.

I got his bottle of perfume and it must have cost him a small fortune. I'm delighted you will be able to obtain the steward's job for Sam Teeling. Fourteen mouths are quite a number to have to feed. I told Bridgie the good news and she's saying a novena for you. Sam is praying, too, that you'll head the poll. 'I wish I had a thousand votes,' he said. 'I'd give them all to Tull.'

Mick is all right, reasonably dependable, but he fecked a fiver out of the till while I was having lunch yesterday. I followed him and made him put it back. He denied it black and blue at first but I searched him and found it in his breast pocket. I gave him a pound. That should keep him going for a day or two. The new girl is dead keen on him but she is sensible. Thanks be to God for that. The patient upstairs would want seven nurses to see her wants. She never stops calling. I turn on the transistor now since it's the only way to drown her out.

Uncle Tom broke out last night and I'd swear Mick was drinking with him. His eyes were bloodshot this morning and he couldn't eat his breakfast. I'll split Uncle Tom when I meet him. Mick is bad enough without turning to the booze. Wait a minute! Here's a telegram and it's from Cork. I'm half afraid to take it. Hooray! Hooray! Hooray! He's passed! You Merciful God, he's passed his exam! I'll tell the countryside. I'll

close, Daddy. Isn't it marvellous? Oh, it's the sweetest
news we ever had. God bless him! God bless him!

Love,
Kate.

Biddy MacAdoo writes to her husband:

Dear Tull,
So-called husband that has his shoes polished in the
best hotels and nothing to worry him, with the health
of a mountain ram. I'm hardly able to hold the pen in
my hand, my nerves are so bad from constant irritation
and dyspepsia and neuritis. There's a tingle now in my
spine often that'd drive any normal woman insane except myself.

What's this I read about James Flannery? When I
opened the paper I nearly dropped dead inside in
my sick bed. I always knew you would bring disgrace
on top of us but this is the biggest disgrace of all. You
always swore to me that there was a battle fought in
Glenalee. You said yourself you wounded two Tans although the Tans denied ever being near Glenalee.
What are we going to do at all. This will be the death
of me. God take me out of my pain and relieve my
suffering. I spilt a nineteen and sixpenny bottle of medicine all over you. I'm not eating a bite. I threw up
rashers and liver. I couldn't keep it down or does
anyone know what I'm going through, even my own
husband with his shoes polished above in the poshest
hotel in Dublin like a Canon or a P.P. No one thinking
about me or will I be taken away in the end when my
senses are gone to a nursing home or does the great
Tull the T.D., the brandy-nose, forget who his wife is

and what ails her. Mick, my own dear son, is a great consolation to me. There's money missing out of my handbag and he's investigating it. Somebody must have come into the room while I was asleep, he said. How would I know and I in the height of agony. Now I know what Our Saviour went through in the Garden of Eden. I wish I was surrounded by serpents the way I feel. And now James Flannery finding out about you to crown my misfortune. We'll be disgraced and Mick going to be a doctor. What patients will come to him, I tell you, after this except the riff-raff. He'll get none of the priests anyway and no convent would let him near them when his father is found out.

I'm starting another novena for you to know would God in his mercy take pity on you and save you from the powers of the devil, that Flannery, that schoolmaster with his row of Biros in his pocket and the tweed suit to crown it. The Latin should be read over that fellow and sprinkled after it in public. The hand is tired. God forgive you.

Your wife,
Biddy.

Tull MacAdoo writes to his daughter, Kate:

Dublin.

My dear Kate,
That's great news entirely about Mick. It's almost too good to be true. You're sure, I suppose, that it wasn't some other Mick MacAdoo? I'm only joking! It's the biggest surprise since Delaney won the gold medal in Australia. I'm going out to-night with Mac and the two of us will get plastered on the strength of it.

Now, Kate, I made Mick a promise. I told him that if he ever passed that confounded exam, I would stand him a holiday in Ballybunion, but he seemed to prefer Bundoran. Every man to his taste, as the saying goes. I was never a man to go back on my word, whatever my other failings may have been. I want you to outfit him like a hotel manager and give him fifty pounds and also the price of a return train ticket to Bundoran. The poor fellow deserves it after all the doubts we had about him. How did your mother take it? Maybe it will get her out of the bed, if such a thing is possible, which I doubt very much indeed.

The second thing I want you to do is to check with oul' Willie Blakeney of Blakeney's Cross about the number of wynds in the two meadows. Find out from him if they are as big as last year and how many wynds there are. I'll need a lot of hay this winter as I intend going in for store cattle. Beef will be high next summer. There is a whisper here about a new agreement with Great Britain.

That's terrible bloody news about Flannery, but not as bad as it sounds. I doubt if he'll go any farther when you hear what I have to say. The moment I got your letter, I brought Mac into the resident's lounge here at MacMell's, opened a bottle of brandy and locked the door from the inside. Mac's first idea was to get sworn statements from the survivors of the battle, but, since there are no survivors, this would not be possible. He suggested we invent survivors and he could get a friend of his to draw up the necessary statements. This friend got four years for forgery some time ago but he's all right now and looking for an honest day's work. There's none of us perfect.

I think you will agree that Mac's idea was a good one, but mine is better as I know certain things that nobody else knows. We will have to move fast, however, before this thing gets out of hand and, since I cannot come down to Tourmadeedy at the moment, I am leaving everything in your hands. I trust you completely.

Follow carefully. The third thatched house on the bohareen that goes over Crabapple Hill is occupied by a woman called Jenny Jordan, two doors down from Kane's place. You know where Crabapple Hill is, but in case you don't, it is seven miles north of Kilnavarna and there's a signpost where the bohareen meets the main road. Jenny Jordan is a useful friend of mine and will do anything for me. I got her an I.R.A. pension ten years ago, which she deserved. She was no Countess Markievicz but she often carried a dispatch in her bloomers and many's the time she brought ammunition from Kilnavarna to Tourmadeedy. She is a good oul' soul and she'll like you instantly when she hears you are my daughter.

Go to see her at once. Do not delay a minute.

Here is the twist in the story. Thirty years ago before Flannery married, Jenny Jordan worked for him as a housekeeper. The inevitable happened and she had a baby daughter whom she called Maud, after Maud Gonne.

Flannery sent her to England – where they all go. She stayed there a year, supported by Flannery. I know he's an unhung scoundrel but he was never mean with money. Jenny came home after the birth and left the baby to be adopted. Flannery settled a hundred pounds on her (worth about six hundred to-day) and there was no more about it. The only persons who know this are Flannery and Jenny, yours truly and now yourself. Oul' Canon Murkason knew about it, too, but he kept it under his hat and wherever he is the secret is gone with him.

Flannery doesn't know that I know. You see, Kate, my darling, there are lots of things I know about people, necessary things in case I ever need them. It's part and parcel of the dirty game we call politics. Don't ever judge a politician outright if he does something which seems underhand. He is only doing his best to survive. Anyhow, between the jigs and the reels, Flannery married Elsie Rice (a grade A snob) who taught in the school with him. Elsie was always a girl who thought her water was Eau de Cologne.

They had four kids, as you know. There's the solicitor. There's the daughter who married the doctor in Ballybobawn. There's the dentist in Kilnavarna and, finally, there's the curate in Cloghauneen parish down south. Explain to Jenny what Flannery is trying to do to me. Point out to her that I might well lose my seat if his ugly lies began to snowball. Get her to go to Flannery and tell him that, unless he publishes an apology, she will make the affair of the child known. He must come to his knees. It will wreck his whole family unless he does and if he doesn't, I'm ruined. Get her to go to him without delay and everything should be rosy in the garden.

There is another woman, married now in Tobergorm, whom he is supposed to have sired but I am not sure about this. Flannery's great weakness was that he was a bit of a ram and I've yet to hear tell of a cautious ram and I'm prepared to swear that I've seen Flannery's long nose and big ears on a dozen kids, although I couldn't prove it if I was asked.

Well, Kate darling, I leave you to it. I hope to God Jenny succeeds in frightening him. If she fails, I don't know what I'll do, although I don't think she's likely to fail. Flannery has too much to lose, what with his son a curate and the wife and all, not to mention the pupils and the new Canon. The new Canon has no time for rams. I will now conclude, darling Kate, and I look forward eagerly to hearing from you. You might say that my whole future depends on you.

Love,
Daddy.

P.S. I went to confession to Father Flannery once when I was serving in a bye-election. (Flannery's son, Father Jack, as they call him down there.) You couldn't meet a nicer confessor, not if you went to poor Pope John himself. But I have to live, too, and I have you and your mother and Mick to think about and Henry on top of you. Mac sends you his love as always. If Mac wasn't stuck in politics he would be a saint. He would do anything for a friend.

Love,
Dad.

Kate MacAdoo writes to her father:

My darling Daddy,
Don't worry! Remember those words. Don't worry. Everything will be taken care of and you'll head the poll, no bother. Henry is here with me at the moment and he is giving me the loan of his car to go to Crab-apple Hill. He doesn't know what it's all about and he isn't curious. He is a wonderful person. All that concerns him is my happiness. He'll make a good hubby.

I'll contact Jenny Jordan straightaway and let you have a full report of all activities the moment anything conclusive occurs which should be at the precise moment she puts her cards on the table before Flannery. I knew you would come up with something. Tell Mac he's a genius, that I wouldn't dream of having anybody else for a godfather.

I've given Mick the money, and the money for a new outfit, too. When I come back from Crabapple Hill, Henry will drive him to the station. Mick is a new man since he passed. He's beginning to look and act like a fully-fledged doctor. He is meeting a bunch of fellow-students in Bundoran, so it should be lively up there. Let us hope it will not be too lively. We both know Mick. A bill has arrived from his landlady in Cork for six week's lodgings. I expected it.

Mother is much the same – no improvement but no deterioration either. We both know there's nothing the matter with her, but we must put up with it, mustn't we? I won't dilly-dally with more news. There's a job to be done and I'm the woman to do it. I'm going straight to Crabapple Hill, or – if you like – to Flannery's unveiling. I always suspected he was a bit of a boyo. He pinched my behind once at a social.

Above all, Daddy, you're not to worry about it. Have no doubts but that my next letter will be laden with good news and the mouth of one James Flannery N.T. will be sealed unto infinity. He knows where he stands and he daren't do anything now. Remember not to worry.

'Bye, Daddy, and don't worry.
Love,
Kate.

CHAPTER EIGHT

Mick MacAdoo writes to his father:

Bundoran.

Dear Dad,

Weather wonderful here with balmy breezes, fine-looking women, and all that. A great place to develop an appetite but the food is expensive. In fact, so is everything. It should be an easy passage to the Finals, so you had better become accustomed to calling me Doctor. Money simply evaporates here, although this is only my second day. I paid my hotel bill in advance, £24. I was wondering if you would be good enough to send a few extra quid, say fifteen or even twenty if you can manage. I'll pay it all back to you when you fix me up with a good dispensary some day. Send it as soon as possible as I'm tied to my room without a penny in my pocket. I spent my last sixpence on a blade. I haven't had a smoke in hours. You would think Kate might have stuck a few cartons of cigarettes into my suitcase, but trust your Kate to do the right thing.

Love,
Mick.

Dublin.

Dear Mick,
At this particular time I consider it most unfair of you
to burden me with your financial worries. I have
enough troubles of my own but I have no notion of
transferring them to you as I want you to enjoy your
holiday. If you would only think about other people
and not always be putting yourself first. You're never
done with begging.

You should have studied Economics, not Medicine.
You're the best warrant I ever knew to screw money
out of a person. Kate gave you fifty pounds and your
return fare – and already you want more. However,
I suppose I can't be too hard on you. You will find my
cheque for fifteen pounds enclosed. Holy Mother,
fifteen pounds, imagine! It would support a labouring
man and his family for two weeks or are you aware
of these things at all. I never had a holiday in my life.
When I was your age I spent the fifteenth of August
in Ballybunion. If I had sixpence for seagrass and
periwinkles I was lucky.

Go easy with your spending and go easy with the
girls. When your holiday is over I'll get you on as a
temporary timekeeper on the Awnee Drainage Scheme.
Ten quid a week and damn all to do only make certain your watch is in good order – or have you got a
watch? You will enjoy the characters working on the
scheme. There's oul' Micky Byrne (Tricky Micky, we
call him). Would you believe it that when I told him
there would be bulldozers on the river bank, he told
me that he always thought a bulldozer was a cow that

fell asleep when there was a bull around. You'll really enjoy yourself but it's imperative that you stay awake. There will be enough sleeping on the job without the timekeeper starting it. I don't want any girls around either while you're working. 'Twould be the last straw if you did damage.

Seriously now, son, I want no more requests for money. I have enough worries with the general election drawing near and I have one major worry at this time which could be disastrous but, like I said, I want you to enjoy your holiday. It could be your last one if things go wrong.

I'll close now, as I have an unopened letter here from your mother which I must read and answer so as to have it ready for the morning's post. Enjoy yourself and be sure not to miss Mass. It's all we have, you know – the Faith. Lose it and you lose all. Write to your mother at the first opportunity. Write her a long, funny letter as she needs a lot of cheering up. Drop a card to Kate and to Henry and drop a few cards to as many people you can in the constituency. Votes are votes and I enclose a pound's worth of stamps for the cards. Enjoy yourself and don't do anything I wouldn't do.

Love,
Dad.

Biddy MacAdoo writes to her husband:

Dear Tull,
It's ages since you wrote a line to me and I here in bed with my nerves in a bad state and my left breast sore. Maybe 'tis cancer I'm getting or maybe 'tis some-

thing worse altogether. There is no disease going but doesn't pay me a visit or how does one human body endure it all. Will you tell me that? You sitting down in fine health in Dail Eireann and me here on my last legs thrown down on the bed. God help me, I'm to be pitied and no word from you to find out if I'm dead or alive or do you care what becomes of me above there and you surrounded by luxury and your meals served up to you by waiters in white coats. There was a time, and I young and plump, that you never left my side.

I suppose 'tis boozing on brandy you are with that fecker McFillen. He's not fit company for any one and if you knew some of the yarns I heard about that fellow, you would say hell wasn't hot enough for him. He's the talk of all holy Catholic mothers and their innocent daughters. Books wouldn't give down the tales about him. Mick passed his exam. I barely saw him at all on account of you and the fifty pounds you gave him to go to Bundoran. I do like to be beside the seaside. 'Tis far away from the seaside we are, God bless us and save us in the warm weather. Far away indeed from the time I was a slip of a girl walking the streets of Ballybunion in my figure and you winking at me. That's forgot now, is it, Tull? 'Tis me should be going to Bundoran and you needn't mind writing back to say you'll send me as it's too late now anyway. I wouldn't be able for it. I wouldn't be able to travel three times around the house without a black sweat breaking out through me. 'Tis to Lourdes I should be going with a private nurse and a wheelchair. I see where the Minister's wife got an audience with the Pope. I never even had an audience with a bishop, not to mind a pope and imagine I a T.D.'s wife or does the T.D. think about me at all, or maybe there's another woman in the T.D.'s mind whose wife is a pity and a martyr to her nerves. I hear Dublin is surrounded by prostitutes, black and all sorts of colours, and houses with the women going around with nothing on them except garters and head--carves to tease the young men. Scurrilous is what it is, scurrilous conduct in a Catholic country. There's nuns or no one safe the way people are carrying on.

Isn't it lucky I'm in my bed? You'd think Mick would stay a few days after passing his exam but no, he's off to Bundoran. Off to Bundoran and his poor mother with no one to talk to and her only son that was the difficult rearing with mumps and scarlatina gone off to the seaside instead of staying at home nursing his victim of a mother. There's two charms gone off my bracelet. I wouldn't say I lost them. I hope he's not flogging them off in some pawnshop. The nice rearing he turned out to be – my own flesh and blood. 'Tis from the MacAdoo's he brought it, not from our side, that's certain and sure I may tell you. Fifty pounds no less and when I wanted a new lavatory put up the time Father O'Donnell was coming home I had to go down on my knees to you for a few hundred pounds. My breast is agonising and little you care or do you know you have a wife and mother of your family at all?

I won't be here for the October elections, making tea and firing whiskey into your friends. I'll be above in Lisdoonvarna, D.V., with Maggie Simpson. The two of us have it planned to go if my nerves improve, or is this new attack to be the finish of me? Lisdoonvarna is the last hope for me or do you begrudge me even that? I can't bear it and I eat only a few bites yesterday, and you guzzling chickens and what not up in MacMell's, and other things maybe, behind my back. Sometimes I wish for death to bring relief to my sufferings and what harm but I the most religious woman in Ireland that never missed her Nine Fridays when she had her health, that never did a bad thing to any one or even only had the good word as them that know me will swear in the high court of law. Why is it always the good ones that suffer, or is that the way that God has it planned for us. 'Tis our cross, I dare-say, and the cross must be borne by the humble and the suffering and the lamenting in this vale of tears.

Your wife,
Biddy.

Mick MacAdoo writes to his mother:

Bundoran.

My dear Mother,
Having a grand time here but it's spoiled a lot knowing how much you are suffering. You're a saint, a pure saint, the way you put up with it. Wait till I'm qualified and the two of us will go to Lourdes. I'll be acting as your personal physician. We'll have a rare old time between us. I visit the chapel regularly to say a prayer that your health might improve, and please God it will. There are new drugs coming on the market every day and who knows but one of these days some chemist will come up with an all-purpose drug to suit you. We will get it at cost price since I am in the medical trade so you see it's worth while having a son who is a doctor.

By the way, mother, a small request. I gave an African Missionary here a few pounds to say Masses for you. I did it on impulse and now I find that I have only ten shillings left to my name. Is there any chance you could send me ten pounds without letting Kate know about it. It will only be a loan and I will pay you back on the treble when I'm qualified. Better still if you could send £12 as I promised a Lord's daughter from England that I would take her to a dress dance and the tickets are £1 each so the extra £2 would cover the cost of the tickets. This is a very nice girl and she often enquiries about you although she's English and titled. I make out that the richer people are, the nicer they are. I have her saying a few prayers for you, too.

The weather is quite good here and I spend most of the day on the strand. I'm in bed every night at 10.30. I don't go to the dances like the other fellows as I'm short of money. The hotel bill alone will be up to £40, a small fortune. I've given up smoking and I hadn't a drink since I came.

Send the £12 by return of post if at all possible as I really need it.

> Your loving son,
> Mick.

Kate MacAdoo writes to her father:

My dear Daddy,
There was a letter from Bundoran this morning with curt instructions for the dispatch of twenty-five pounds as your beloved son expressed his intentions of spending a third week there. He didn't even say 'please'. I sent him a telegram telling him where to get off and ordering him home at once. He immediately sent another telegram saying he was in dire straits for cash so I wired him fifty shillings which was quite enough for him. He must be boozing like a fish up there.

Now for the joyful part. I went to Crabapple Hill to see Jenny Jordan and she received me with open arms. She was so excited when I told her who I was. She dabbed her eyes with a handkerchief whenever your name was mentioned and she bawled out crying a few times when I told her that you had such a very high opinion of her. You certainly have a loyal friend on Crabapple Hill and make no mistake about it. Anyhow I put the facts of the case before her and at first she was reluctant but with a bit of pressure she agreed.

I took her in the car to Kilnavarna and on the way into the village who should we see walking along the road, swinging his walking-cane, but the great schoolmaster himself, wearing a white straw hat if you don't mind and a most impressive row of fountainpens, biros and pencils adorning his waistcoat pocket. You will have to agree that he is a fine-looking man, well-preserved and of most commanding appearance.

I pulled up and told him that Jenny wanted to speak to him. He grew flustered and tongue-tied and tried to brazen his way out of it by walking away from us, and a grand majestic way he has of walking. I followed him in the car and shouted through the window at him:

'Walk away if you like,' I said; 'Your wife will do just as well.'

'Wait a minute!' he whispered. 'Leave my wife out of this.'

I swear to God, Daddy, I never saw anyone so terrified, and for a minute I felt sorry for him — but only for a minute, because I remembered what he was trying to do to you. But honestly I felt for him because he knew he was up to his ears in trouble. But it was Tull MacAdoo or James Flannery and that was that.

'Get out,' he said to me, 'and I'll talk to Miss Jordan in the car.' He stood very aloof then and fingered his moustache. I must say that he recovered his composure immediately and I'm sure he felt that he was master of the situation again. God pity him! He didn't know the power of Tull MacAdoo's influence.

I obliged and went for a walk along the road. There was nobody in sight. An hour passed and I got impatient but Flannery made no move to leave. I signalled to him that I wouldn't wait any longer. He pulled down the window and asked me to give him ten minutes. He was as pale as a corpse and the jauntiness gone from him and he chain-smoked the whole time he was in the car. Another half-hour passed and finally he got out. He didn't look at me when he passed me by. All he said was: 'Tull never heard of the Marquis of Queensbury'.

Jenny Jordan was crying her eyes out when I got into the car. It took her a long time to come back to herself but when she did she disclosed the following facts.

Flannery tried everything in his power to force her to remain silent. He explained about his wife and family and what it would mean if they ever found out. He mentioned his son, the curate, but Jenny held firm. In the end he offered her £250 but she told him that all he had to do was to withdraw publicly what he said about you. He started off again about his wife and family and told her you were a scoundrel and a gangster.

'Ah, but, Master,' she pointed out to him, 'hasn't poor oul' Tull a wife and family too. If your wife and family found out wouldn't you still have your job, but if you published the lies about Tull couldn't he be out of a job?'

Flannery tried every trick he knew for a solid hour and a half, and when all fruit failed he tried to buy her with the money. The upshot of the meeting is that an unqualified apology will appear in next week's paper and so all is well and your honour is no longer threatened.

I will tell you one thing I learned and it is a rather strange thing. Jenny Jordan still loves Flannery. Imagine still being in love with him after all these years and after what he did to her. He must have been quite a man in his day. It's a pity he's opposed to you. He would make an excellent Senator on appearance alone. Then that deep booming voice of his would be another asset.

Now for some bad news. Uncle Tom is on the jigs from whiskey. He spent two days boozing in Kettleton's Bar in Kilnavarna and when he fell off into a sleep, Mr and Mrs Kettleton took him upstairs and put him into bed. They sent for me and I went upstairs to the room. I took his shoes, clothes, hat, everything and locked him in.

What do you think he did? He found a white shift belonging to Mrs Kettleton in the wardrobe and put it on. He climbed out the window and down the eaves-shoot. How he wasn't killed is a mystery to me. Sergeant Keogh caught him going into another pub and took him back to Kettleton's. Luckily only a few old women saw him. It was dark and they thought he was a ghost. One of them fainted and had to be given brandy. I made Uncle Tom go down on his knees and promise me on the bible that he would not touch another drop of whiskey for the rest of his life. If he stuck to the few pints, all would be fine; but the whiskey puts him on the jigs. I'll close now, Daddy. Henry sends his regards and mother is still in bed. I hope you're taking care of yourself. Didn't I tell you that all would be well. You can't whack the MacAdoo's when they put up a united front. Even the cunning of James Flannery will not prevail against them. Give my love to Mac and tell him I have his room ready.

Love,
Kate.

CHAPTER NINE

Tull MacAdoo writes to his daughter, Kate:

Dublin.

My dear Kate,
Thanks be to the Holy God Above that Flannery is
going to make apology in the paper. The worry of
him had the sleep robbed from me and I was in a
queer way, I may tell you. I swear to you that I would
be worse than your Uncle Tom in the end because if
Flannery succeeded I would seek release in the whiskey bottle. God bless you, Kate. You conducted yourself better than I ever expected and thanks to you my
good name is safe.

Your mother is writing strange letters to me. She is
a very demanding woman – always was although she
wouldn't admit that part of it to-day. She says she
intends going to Lisdoonvarna for the October elections, Lisdoonvarna of all places, when the constituency
will be like a beehive. Kate, love, I hate asking you to
do this, but is there any chance you could postpone
your wedding until the elections are over. You *don't*
have to do it and it isn't fair to Henry or yourself but,
quite frankly, I couldn't go it alone again. Your
mother was nearly the death of me the last time. Do
you remember the night she put on the accent when
the Minister's wife came in for a cup of coffee. God
forgive me – 'tis wrong to be talking about her – but
she thinks of nobody but herself. I decided not to
answer the last letter she wrote. Shakespeare himself
couldn't answer it.

If she would only behave like other women and give me a minute's peace. If she was one bit predictable itself. I'm sure she would love to be hobnobbing with royalty and ministers and bishops but I wouldn't get many votes if I hung around with the big shots. They would start saying that my success was gone to my head. Talk to her, Kate, and try to drive some commonsense into her. She's beyond me. She seems to find satisfaction in needling me. I have been a great husband to her. I've supported all belonging to her for years without a word of complaint. I gave her father ('Oul' Scutter Heels') three hundred pounds to buy two fields in Glenalee. All her nieces are telephonists and I've forgotten how many of her nephews I've got into the Guards and, if you don't mind, one of her nephews, a Sergeant, stopped me once to ask me for my tax. 'Shag off!' says I to him, 'or I'll have you transferred to the Blasket Islands.' You have no idea of the number of letters I receive every week from your mother's relations – all looking for something: money or jobs or both. Kate, I often think that if I met another woman, more suited to me, a normal wife, that I might have been a better man.

About the wedding – postpone it if you can and you won't be sorry. I'll settle a good penny on you the morning of your marriage. For the present, God bless.

All my love,
Daddy.

P.S. I should be home next week. The session is about to close before the elections.

James Flannery, N.T. writes to Tull MacAdoo, T.D.:
National School.

Dear Tull,

I've just had a session with Jenny Jordan concerning a very human indiscretion committed a long, long time ago. The apology will appear in next week's paper and it should satisfy you. You are a shoddy man, Tull, and a crafty man and you know as well as I do that there was never a Battle of Glenalee. There was a one-sided battle all right on the night yourself and Razzy murdered the Sergeant, an unfortunate wretch who was only carrying out his duty and carrying it out rather indifferently at that. Can you explain how no Black and Tan or member of the British Military was killed by you and your so-called fighting men when in every other part of the country they were fighting tooth and nail for a cause that meant death.

Poor Jenny Jordan. Don't you think, Tull, that I often stay awake nights, haunted by the awful fact that there is a child of mine somewhere in England, a young man who is my son and about whom I know nothing. My worst punishment is that I cannot do a dam thing about him. I cannot search for him, and I cannot forget him. I was a young man then, Tull, and young men are virile and hungry. They must be forgiven a lot. Do you ever blush, Tull, when you remember the past or does the past mean anything to you?

There is a stain or two in every man's yesterdays. Mine is Jenny Jordan and a few other women – with others I was lucky. Yours are the Battle of Glenalee, the killing of that defenceless sergeant and the others that only you know about. You are not a fair fighter, Tull. I will concede that a professional politician cannot afford to be, but to defile the basic principles of co-existence by exposing the human failings of a fellow human being is stooping a little too low. However, I have long ago convinced myself that nothing is beyond you when your alleged good name is at stake. How I wish that I were free of responsibility. If I were, I would break you, but you know as well as I do that I am reduced, by you, to the stature of a helpless old man.

Neither you nor I are greedy men, Tull, and we are both reasonably charitable. As a human being, I could probably like you, but as a politician you stink with an odour so putrid that my stomach revolts at the most insignificant of your actions. I got to be a teacher on merit, and merit alone, and you got to be a member of the Dail on merit, a particular kind of merit, yet you consistently betray the trait that made you successful.

To you, Tull, nothing is sacred – not even the dignity of your own daughter, whom you profess to love. You have made her share some of the vileness of your own responsibility. Funnily enough, I liked her because of her intense loyalty to you. For what you have done, you will both suffer yet, she in particular – or do you understand me? I think you do.

The main point I would like to make in this letter, Tull, is that you have corrupted everything you touched. You have damaged everything irrevocably. My only satisfaction is that you are part of the slime which surrounds you. Your legacy will be your ignorance, your crudity and your villainy.

James Flannery, N.T.

Tull MacAdoo, T.D. answers James Flannery, N.T.:

Dublin.

Dear Ram:

Listen, Flannery, or should I call you Archangel Flannery? Perhaps I should call you Excellency. It's the sort of salute you expect. Well, you're not dealing with schoolchildren now, Master Flannery. You're dealing with Tull MacAdoo, a grown man who doesn't give a tinker's curse about you. Another reference to my daughter and I'll blow your brains out. Worse still, I might beat you till you hadn't a breath of life left in you. Now you're trying to tell me that it's unnatural for a daughter to want to help her own father. Well, let me tell you, it's the most natural thing in the world. Your own actions prove it. You firmly believe there was no Battle of Glenalee and you say you can prove it. But you daren't prove it, Flannery, out of loyalty to your own family, or maybe it's fear of your own family. You don't want to hurt them. Please remember that my daughter doesn't want to see me hurt either. And, above all, I don't want to see her hurt. God have mercy on the soul of the man who offends her.

But, of course, you and your family are different — special! Who are you trying to kid! It must be yourself. Yes, that's it! You're kidding yourself. You and your stupid principles: principles, moryah, and principles when they suit you, but only when they suit you. Wouldn't a man of principle have married Jenny Jordan in the first place and say to hell with the neighbours and public opinion. But not you, Principles Flannery, the worthy schoolmaster.

Listen, Flannery! Why don't you go for the Dail? You have a following who think you're God Almighty.

You would definitely get in. No bloody fear, Flannery: you leave the dirty work to me and my equals and criticize us with safety from a distance.

You're an educated man, Flannery, and I'm surprised that you don't know more about yourself. I'll tell you exactly what you are, for nothing. You're a cod, Flannery, a pompous oul' cod who never did anything in his life except to criticize when you know it will cost you nothing and when there's no danger in it.

What did you do for the country if you're so concerned about it? Did you ever run for the County Council? If things are as rotten as you say, isn't it the duty of an educated man to stand up and protest? Why don't you do something positive? Don't say that you can't because of Jenny Jordan. You had thirty free years to do something constructive and when you try to do something after your own heart – something destructive – you haven't the courage to go through with it. You spineless, pitiful fool. 'Tis the likes of you that has this country held back with your weak whispers and rumours, terrified of your bloody lives and jobs to come out in the open.

What do you know about politics? I don't tell you how to run your school, do I? You'd perish inside of a year if you were stuck in politics. You're not tough enough and you know it. A man has to have the skin of a crocodile if he wants to survive in politics.

You haven't the strength or the courage, Flannery. But, don't worry – I'll carry on and you can be assured of your salary and pension while you have people like Tull MacAdoo holding the country together in spite of you.

Cheerio,
Tull.

Biddy MacAdoo writes to her husband:

Dear Tull,
Loving so-called husband and backbiter that had my
own daughter, my own flesh and blood, giving out the
pay about me. How long is the conspiracy going on?
Do you want me out of the way so bad? So you're
coming down next week, and no word to me, or am I
only a servant girl or a playabout woman to be put
away when your pleasure is done after I bearing you
children through thick and thin when there was no
maternity homes or drugs to kill the pain. I suppose
you're enjoying your four-course dinner and your
soup before it and your sweet after. You were always
a good head to your belly, or anything that gave you
pleasure. You didn't show much control. I suppose
McFillen is telling the dirty, filthy stories as usual.
Well, he'll tell me no more because I'll throw the holy
water on him if he comes within an asses' roar of me.
I had a lovely letter from Mick, three packed pages,
not like you. I sent him a few pounds. He'll only be
young once. He's a good boy only for ye all being
down on him so much. He reminds me a lot of my
father, the same slow smile and the same thoughtful
face by him. A pity my poor father wasn't alive to-day
to see him and to see my suffering here in the bed.

Of course you prefer your little pet of a daughter
who gave out stink to me this morning and wanted me
to shift myself and my bed and I in the throes of mor-
tal suffering. I didn't like to say anything, although I
could say plenty about the Protestants that won't even
believe that there's an Our Lady, our beautiful Bless-
ed Mother, the spouse of St. Joseph and the Mother

78

of God. Did I ever think that I would live to see the day that the daugther I breast-fed would be half a Protestant. The parsons won't be long getting after the children if they have them. You'll have to get out the gun to see they are baptised in the Holy Catholic Church or will they be half and half, with some Catholics and more Protestants. I knew a woman that committed suicide over she changing the faith. Thanks be to God, there's no fear of Mick, my own boy, that will marry a pure clean Catholic girl when he's a doctor. Georgina Muldowney is a nice girl, an only daughter. She called to see me last week and landed a big bag of pears and oranges up on the bed to me. More than my own ever did, after they being the whole cause of the way I am. Do you think of me at all or even when you say your prayers a person would think that your conscience would move you and that you might remember to think that you have a wife who gave the best years of her mortified life to you and yours. May God forgive you.

Your wife.

Tull MacAdoo writes to his wife, Biddy:

Dublin.

My dear Biddy,
What's wrong with my own girl that I love. Why are you so cross with me, or what did I ever do to you only to give you anything you ever wanted. Now, isn't that true? Did I ever refuse you a single thing, or was I ever demanding of you? You'll have to admit that I was always a reasonable man. Ask me to do anything for you and I will do it but don't ask me to give up

politics because I'm good at them and I can do a lot for poor people.

I'll be home next week and maybe the two of us will go off for a few days somewhere. How would you like Killarney? We could spend a few nice nights there in a good hotel, away from it all. I sincerely hope that you will be up and about when I come home. It would be great if we could spend a few days together. and Killarney is beautiful this time of the year. If you say the word, I'll book a double room in the best hotel. It would be a break for me, too, before the elections. I would come back refreshed for the fray. We could do a bit of motoring during the day, see the sights, hire a boat and have a journey over the lakes. I think you'll agree that we should have a most enjoyable time. Write soon, love, and let me know what you think. We fixed Mr Flannery all right.

Ever and always,
Your own Tull.

Biddy MacAdoo writes to her husband:

Tull MacAdoo,
So that's your plan for me, is it? Killarney! Don't you know that I know there's a mental home in Killarney? You covered it nicely with the idea for the double room in the hotel.

Is it a girl of sixteen you think you're playing with? 'Twould be more in your line to forget about going for the Dail again and stay here at home in Tourmadeedy and look after your wife. Everyone that comes to see me tells me that I look desperate bad. The breast is painful and I have neuritis. Soup and toast and a few tit-bits is all I can take now.

I'm taking a tonic, too, that Johnny O'Dell, the chemist in Kilnavarna, made up for me. Sixteen and six for a small bottle but he says 'tis good and he says it brought great relief to the Sergeant's wife the time she lost the child. I eat a slice of brown bread now and then and I'm taking honey for my throat. I had another letter from Mick for a few pounds. He met a Lord's daughter up there and she had her purse whipped from her by Teddy-boys. Mick gave her what he had and was left with nothing himself. This Lord's daughter is from England and they're millionaires over there and she asked Mick over for a holiday. She is an only daughter, too. She's mad about Mick. I'm saying a novena to know would my health ever come back to me. If God listens to prayers, He must have heard a great share of mine. I'm never done praying for all of ye. What about Kathleen Stack's son and the promise you made about getting him into the cadets? She's a good friend and she would cut off her right arm for me. I see in to-day's paper where James Flannery apologises to you about the Battle of Glenalee. He's a right mongrel, that Flannery, and his wife thinks she's a duchess or something. The airs and graces of that one and she going up the aisle of the Church on Sunday are enough to sicken a person. You might think she would show some respect in the house of God. It's a pity some one don't write her an anonymous letter about James and the days he spent rutting the countryside. That wouldn't be long knocking the gumption out of her. There should be a lot more letters to a lot of other high and mighty women around here. There's one doctor's wife playing golf that I could mention and other big shots drinking gin and lime and what nots like that. Ah, no respect for God or man. I'm exhausted now from writing this. I'll end.

Your wife, Biddy.

P.S. Rex Feckler was in to know would you fix him up as an auxiliary postman for the Tubbertone area. There's five more in for it but Rex is deserving. He brought me a fine pair of chickens, plucked and all, when he heard I was knocked up. He always gave you the number one and he always canvassed for you. 'Twas him flung the bicycle tube across the wires the night the opposition had the big meeting. Apart from that, his mother and myself are connected. Her father and my father were third cousins.

Biddy.

Tull MacAdoo writes to his wife, Biddy, who is in Lisdoonvarna:

Dear Biddy,
I trust this finds you well. Give my regards to Maggie. Well, the campaign is nearly ended and the voting commences at 8 o'clock to-morrow morning. I'm nearly exhausted but it's a blessing to me that you are improving a bit. I enclose a cheque for £250 in case you're short or would like to buy something for yourself – a dress or a coat, maybe.

I'll be going to bed now as I want to be up bright and early in the morning. Polling begins at 8 o'clock. I have no doubt whatsoever about the outcome but I still have the same old excitement after all these years. There is nothing to beat election fever, win or lose. MacAdoo, the old warhorse, revels in it. He is in the thick of it now and he will emerge at the top of the poll. I'll try to sleep now but it won't be easy with my seat in the balance. God bless you, my darling wife, and may He guard you and improve you so that you will come back to me a better and a healthier woman. I think I'll make a mug of cocoa before I turn in. Looking back over the years I have certainly come a long way and I have an awful lot to be thankful for, more than most men. I worked hard and I had you behind me and I never refused a man a favour whenever it was possible. Good-night. I'll let you know the result first thing to-morrow.

Love,
Tull.

CHAPTER TEN

*Tull MacAdoo writes to his wife, Biddy, in Lisdoon-
varna:*

The Courthouse,

My dear Biddy,
I'm here at the Courthouse and I can't resist the
urge to drop you a line. The votes have been divid-
ed at last and the first count is about to begin. They've
just broken off for lunch and will start immediately
afterwards.

Take a deep breath, because I am the bearer of
great tidings. You will be overjoyed with what I have
to tell you.

I think you should be the first to know what I am
a cast-iron certainty to head the poll. In fact I confi-
dently expect to poll the highest total ever archieved
by anybody in this constituency. You should see the
looks of astonishment on the faces of the opposition.
Flannery had the gall to come to the count and he is as
pale as a ghost. Kate and Mick are here with me and
wish to be remembered. My pad of votes is twice as
high as the nearest rival and I reckon that I should be
returned on the first count with ten or even eleven
thousand first preferences. I rang poor McFillen a few
minutes ago and it looks like as if he'll lose his seat.
I wonder who will be appointed in his stead. It could
be a certain chap who is your husband. Poor McFillen.
I always told him he couldn't have it both ways. I hope
yourself and Maggie are enjoying Lisdoonvarna. I'll
come up to bring you home whenever you say the

word and if there's anything whatever you want, don't hesitate to ring or write. I'll be at home in Tourmadeedy for the next few days at least. I daresay I'll be expected to throw a bit of a shindig to-night. Kate is looking after that for me. We'll bring in all those who worked hard but to-night my house will be open to every man whether they voted for me or not. I'm not a small man and I'm not a begrudging man. Do you need anything. If you do, write at once and its yours. The salary for parliamentary secretary is very attractive. I will buy a little car for you if you would like it and teach you how to drive.

I'm so elated with the results I can hardly write steadily. The most I expected to poll was eight thousand votes but, wonder of wonders, I should have almost 11,000 first preferences. What have I done to deserve it! I had a call from the Minister to find out if there was any news and when I told him, he was delighted. 'Good solid dependable old Tull,' he said. If I'm not made a parliamentary secretary after this there's no justice in the world. The Minister expects to head the poll himself and he was really tickled at my news, especially since I'll bring another man in with me and especially when McFillen is about to depart the scene. I'll fight like a dog to get Mac a seat in the Senate. He deserves it.

Mick goes back to the University to-morrow, a week late, but he worked his head off during the campaign and I'm convinced he got a lot of the younger votes for me this time. I have a wonderful family, I must say, and you yourself the best of them all, my own dear girl.

Big changes from the day I stood for the County Council. Did you ever think that Tull MacAdoo would head the poll or that one day I would be a parliamentary secretary. They would have laughed at the idea, in those days. Aren't you delighted with my achievement? Nobody ever dreamed that any single man could ever poll ten thousand votes in this area. Tull MacAdoo fooled them all and when you consider how I scraped in on the seventh count the first time it is a truly remarkable performance. It's a historic achievement. The thing now is to work hard to stay at the top. There are hundreds of people here congratulating me and I find it difficult to write. The quota is only 6,800 so that Din Stack should get in, no bother, with my surplus votes. He only polled 3,000 votes but this surprise poll of mine gives him a right chance because my surplus should be enough to check him in in the second count. In fact I think we could take it that he's a T.D. already. He's over in a corner crying his eyes out with joy. "Tis all due to you, Tull,' he said a while ago, and I thought he would break my hand with the shaking he gave it. He's still crying with joy but I think that he's fairly boozed. He was up most of the night drinking. He was too nervous to go to bed. Wait till he's been through as many campaigns as I have.

More good news. Rex Feckler will start next Monday as auxiliary postman for the Tubbertone area, so what do you think of the husband who can fix anything for you? I still can't get over my phenomenal votes. I had better close and shake hands with my admirers. There's a crowd cheering now outside the Courthouse., after hearing that I am about to break all records. I wish you could hear it... 'Three cheers for Tull!' they're shouting. 'Three cheers for Tull Mac-Adoo!'

> Good-bye, my darling and God bless you.
> Your devoted and ever-loving husband,
> Tull.

Biddy MacAdoo writes to her husband:

Lisdoonvarna,
Co. Clare.

Dear Tull,
I got your letter, but I seen it in the papers this morning. You must be pleased with yourself but it's only what I expected. There's a priest here in the hotel, on holidays from the African Missions, and he's a great consolation to us. He says Mass every morning and I swear that I would be a total wreck only for him. He's not well himself, the poor man. He's a pure saint if ever I came across one and Maggie says the same thing. We play a few games of whist at night before going to bed and we have our sulphur bath every day. It does seem to be improving me. By the way, there's one thing I must tell you that you must do for me. There's no pots in the rooms here and we are ashamed to ask for one. Maggie is as shy as me. Would you ever get a good enamel pot and wrap it well and post it on to me. 'Tis an afwul trek downstairs to the toilet, so don't forget, and ask Doctor John to post on my prescription for the red nerve tablets as I want to get some from the chemist here. Or is it too much for you to do after I giving you the best years of my life?

Your unfortunate wife,
Biddy.

LETTERS OF A LOVE-HUNGRY FARMER
John B. Keane

John B. Keane has introduced a new word into the English language — 'chastitute'. This is the story of a chastitute, i.e. a man who has never lain down with a woman for reasons which are fully disclosed within this book. It is the tale of a lonely man who will not humble himself to achieve his heart's desire, whose need for female companionship whines and whimpers throughout. Here are the hilarious sex escapades of John Bosco McLane culminating finally in one dreadful deed.

LETTERS OF A MATCHMAKER
John B. Keane

These are the letters of a country matchmaker faithfully recorded by John B. Keane, whose knowledge of matchmaking is second to none.

In these letters is revealed the unquenchable, insatiable longing that smoulders unseen under the mute, impassive faces of our batchelor brethren.

Comparisons may be odious but readers will find it fascinating to contrast the Irish matchmaking system with that of the 'Cumangettum Love Parlour' in Philadelphia. They will meet many unique characters from the Judas Jennies of New York to Finnuala Crust of Coomasahara who buried two giant-sized, sexless husbands but eventually found happiness with a pint-sized jockey from North Cork.